# The Story Girl
### Book 5

*Dedicated to my six grandchildren, the "cousins," especially to Bethany, for whom I began this journey with the "Story Girl" on "The Golden Road," six years ago. I pray all of you will find these stories about the King cousins a wonderful example for you to follow in holiness, purity, and real fun—and help you along your own journey to the heart of God.*

From the author of Anne of Green Gables

# L.M. Montgomery

# The Story Girl
**Book 5**

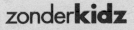

## WINTER ON THE ISLAND

*Adapted by Barbara Davoll*

zonder**kidz**

**zonderkidz.**
The children's group of Zondervan

www.zonderkidz.com

*Winter on the Island*
Copyright © 2005 by The Zondervan Corporation, David Macdonald, trustee and
Ruth Macdonald

Requests for information should be addressed to:
Grand Rapids, Michigan 49530

---

**Library of Congress Cataloging-in-Publication Data**
Davoll, Barbara.
  Winter on the island / by Barbara Davoll ; adapted from The story girl by L.M.
Montgomery.
    p. cm.–(The story girl ; bk. 5)
  Summary: During a winter on Prince Edward Island at the turn of the century, Sara
Stanley--the Story Girl--and the rest of the King cousins start a newspaper, get caught in
a blizzard, receive a visit from the governor's wife, and make New Year's resolutions
  ISBN 10: 0–310–70859–1 (softcover); ISBN 13: 978–0–310–70859–9
  [1. Storytellers—Fiction. 2. Cousins—Fiction. 3. Conduct of
life—Fiction. 4. Prince Edward Island—History—1867-1914—Fiction. 5. Canada
—History—1867-1914—Fiction.] I. Montgomery, L. M. (Lucy Maud), 1874-1942.
Story girl. II. Title.
  PZ7.D3216Wk 2005
  [Fic]--dc22                                                            2004012524

---

Photograph of L. M. Montgomery used by permission of L. M. Montgomery
Collection, Archival and Special Collections, University of Guelph Library.

Zonderkidz is a trademark of Zondervan

*Editor: Amy De Vries*
*Interior design: Susan Ambs*
*Art direction: Merit Alderink*
*Cover illustrations: Jim Griffin*

*Printed in the United States of America*

---

05  06  07 08 /OPM/ 10  9  8  7  6  5  4  3  2  1

# The Story Girl

# Contents

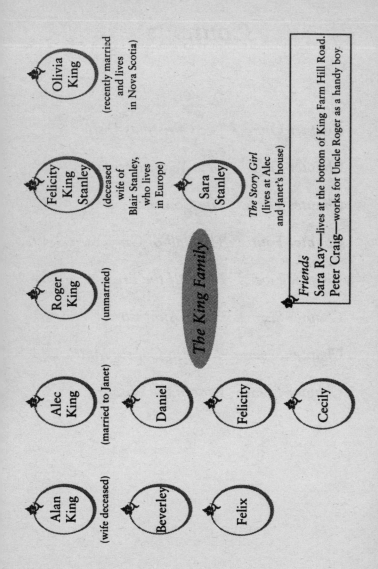

Olivia King (recently married and lives in Nova Scotia)

Felicity King Stanley (deceased wife of Blair Stanley, who lives in Europe)

Sara Stanley *The Story Girl* (lives at Alec and Janet's house)

Roger King (unmarried)

*The King Family*

Alec King (married to Janet)

Daniel

Felicity

Cecily

Alan King (wife deceased)

Beverley

Felix

*Friends*
Sara Ray—lives at the bottom of King Farm Hill Road.
Peter Craig—works for Uncle Roger as a handy boy.

# *The Christmas Harp*

*The harp the young shepherd held began to
play softly by itself. All his secret longings
were expressed in it.*

# *Chapter One*

s Christmas drew near, the King house was full of excitement. My brother Felix and I, who were staying with our King cousins in Father's absence, couldn't believe that we were actually going to be a part of it all. Father had written that he needed us to continue to stay with our family on Prince Edward Island for a few months longer, so he could better establish his business in South America. He wanted to find a more suitable home for us before we joined him.

Secretly we were overjoyed to stay longer with our King cousins, even though we missed Father. He had sent us extra money to purchase Christmas gifts, and we couldn't wait to spend it. Felix and I had just been out shopping in Avonlea. It had been snowing lightly as we went in and out of the gaily-decorated stores, looking for just the right gifts for Father and for our uncles. We figured our girl cousins would help us find presents for our aunts.

We had bought a handsome pocketknife for Uncle Alec, whom we were living with, and a shaving mug and brush with the English flag on it for Uncle Roger.

"Let's run over to Uncle Roger's and show these to Peter," I said excitedly, as we turned onto the lane that led to the farm. "He won't tell anybody what we got them."

Felix agreed and we squeezed through the hedgerow that ran between our farms. Peter, who was Uncle Roger's handy boy, was just coming from the barn and was happy to see us. He worked hard and was always glad for a break.

"Look what we got Uncle Roger and Uncle Alec for Christmas," I said in a low tone. I didn't want to spoil the surprise by letting Uncle Roger or Aunt Olivia, Uncle Roger's sister, hear us.

"That's great, Bev," said Peter with enthusiasm. He and I were best of friends, maybe because he never made fun of my weird name, Beverley. I think he knew how hard it was for me as a boy to have this girlish name. He always called me Bev, which sounded more masculine. Besides, I just plain liked Peter. He was full of fun and was always ready to own up to his pranks when he got caught. He was as much a part of our King family as the rest of us were.

Just then Uncle Roger drove up the lane, coming home from doing some shopping himself. We scattered, hoping the snowfall had kept him from seeing what we were showing Peter. "See you later," we called as we headed back through the hedgerow.

It was such a dream for us two lonely, motherless boys to have a huge family of cousins. Our mother had died when we were very young, and although Father tried hard to make up for that, we had always been quite lonely in Toronto. We had no idea what South America would be like when we moved, but we sure loved it on the Island with our cousins.

For one thing there was the Story Girl, one of our girl cousins, whose real name was Sara Stanley. We called her "The Story Girl" because she was a barrel of fun and had a story for every occasion. She was fourteen and knew a lot of things about girls we needed to learn. Her mother was not living either, so we felt a real bond with her. Her father was an artist who made his living in Paris. He was regarded as the King family "black sheep," but he sounded wonderful to me. He often sent Sara beautiful gifts and treasures from France.

Peter and the Story Girl lived next door with Uncle Roger and Aunt Olivia. Aunt Olivia wasn't Uncle Roger's wife. She was his sister and house-keeper. We loved them both, although Uncle Roger was a terrible tease. Aunt Olivia, the youngest of all our grown-ups, was lots of fun—and beautiful, too.

Our younger cousin, Cecily, was a little sweetie, but we couldn't stand her snooty big sister, Felicity— she was so conceited. (No family is perfect, you know.) Dan, their older brother, was always into some mischief.

Also part of our motley bunch was sad, little Sara Ray, Cecily's best friend, who lived at the bottom of Farm Hill Road. She was a pain and cried all the time, but we included her in most everything. Felix (my pudgy brother) and I rounded out the bunch of crazy cousins. Life was never dull at the King homestead.

Uncle Alec had tired, blue eyes and reminded us of our father. He and his wife, Aunt Janet, were almost perfect. Of course, we were decidedly imperfect, and sometimes they had to get after us. But we loved being part of the King family. And never did it seem more fun than at Christmastime.

The air was filled with secrets. We all had been saving our money for weeks and counting it daily. Homemade dainties were smuggled into hiding places, and whispers behind closed doors were the rule of the day. Nobody even thought of being jealous when they heard the whispers.

Felicity was in her element as she and her mother were making food preparations for the big day. Cecily and the Story Girl were always excluded from this as they weren't cooks, nor did they pretend to be. Nevertheless, their feelings were often hurt by the superior looks Felicity gave them and her snooty behavior. Cecily took this to heart and often complained about it.

"I'm as much a part of this family as Felicity is. I don't think she needs to shut me out of everything. When I wanted to pick the seeds out of the raisins for the mincemeat, she said, 'No, I'll do it myself because Christmas mincemeat is *very* particular.' As if I can't be trusted to stone raisins properly. The airs she puts on about her cooking just makes me sick," she concluded angrily.

"It's a pity she doesn't make a mistake in cooking once in a while. That would bring her down off her high horse," I agreed.

Presents were arriving daily from friends and family. Aunt Janet and Aunt Olivia were taking charge of those, making sure none of us small fry would sneak peek. How slowly the last week had passed. Felix and I sent off gifts to our father—and to tell you the honest truth, we really wished he could have been with us. We loved him and missed him in spite of all the fun.

Even "watched pots finally boil"—meaning that at last, Christmas Eve was upon us and then the day itself. It arrived a bit gray and frostbitten outside, but inside all was rosy red and exciting.

Uncle Roger, Aunt Olivia, and the Story Girl came over early in the morning. Peter came, too. We had all been concerned that he would have to go to his mother's house to spend Christmas. But at the last moment, a cousin in Charlottetown invited Mrs. Craig for Christmas, and Peter was given a choice to go with her or stay with us. Of course he joyfully chose to stay with all of us. So we were all together, except Sara Ray, Cecily's little friend who lived down the hill. Her mother wouldn't let her come.

We had an exciting time opening our presents. Some of us had more than others, but we all received enough so that no one felt neglected. The contents of the box the Story Girl's father sent her from Paris made all of our eyes bulge out.

It was full of beautiful things. One was a red silk dress, not like the other one he had sent her for her birthday. That one was bright, but this one was a rich, dark crimson with bows and ruffles, and there were little red satin slippers to go with it. They had gold buckles and high heels that made Aunt Janet hold up her hands in horror.

Felicity said spitefully that she thought Sara Stanley would get tired of wearing red so much.

"I'd never get tired of red," responded Sara to Felicity. "It's just so rich and glowing. I always feel more clever in red, and the thoughts for my stories come easier than when I'm dressed in other colors."

"Oh, you darling dress—you dear, sheeny, red rosy, glistening, silky thing!" she cried, hugging it to herself and dancing around the kitchen.

The Story Girl also got a present from the Awkward Man—a little shabby, worn book with a great many marks inside it.

"Why it isn't new—it's an old book!" exclaimed Felicity. "I didn't think the Awkward Man was stingy, even if he is awkward." Jasper Dale was a tall, thin man who was often awkward and always shy around ladies.

"Oh, you don't understand, Felicity," said the Story Girl patiently. "I'd ten times rather have this than a new book. It's one of his own, don't you see— one that he's read a hundred times and loved and made a friend of."

Peter was in seventh heaven because Felicity had given him a present—one she had made herself. He was just thrilled that she had made such a special effort.

Even Paddy, the Story Girl's cat, had a blue Christmas ribbon for his neck. He promptly chewed it off and lost it. He had no concern that it was Christmas and that he should be festive.

We had a wonderful Christmas dinner. It was all we had dreamed about, after smelling the glorious smells the whole week. All of us ate 'til we bulged, and in the evening—as though we needed more celebrating—we went to Kitty Marr's party.

It was a lovely December evening. It had warmed up during the day 'til it felt more like fall. There was no snow, but a weird, purple stillness had settled over the hills. Nature seemed to have folded her hands to rest, knowing that the long winter was coming.

When we first got the invitation to go to the party, Aunt Janet said we couldn't go. But Uncle Alec talked her into it. I think Cecily's brown eyes persuaded him. She was his favorite, and he seemed easier on her lately. I noticed him looking at her with concern. Cecily did seem paler and thinner than she had been in the summer. Her soft eyes seemed larger, and she looked tired. Her quiet ways made her seem sweet and pathetic.

I had overheard Uncle Alec remarking to Aunt Janet that Cecily reminded him of his sister, our Aunt Felicity, who had died when she was very young. "I hope Cecily isn't getting sick like Felicity," he said.

"Don't be foolish, Alec! Cecily is perfectly healthy," Aunt Janet snapped, as if that settled the matter. But I did notice after that conversation that Aunt Janet always made sure Cecily wore her boots when she went outside in cold weather and gave her cream to drink when the rest of us had milk.

On this Christmas evening, however, none of us was thinking about anything except having a good time. Cecily looked beautiful with her shining eyes and a nice rosy pink on her cheeks. If we had looked closer, we might have noticed they were more flushed than usual. But we didn't.

Felicity was too beautiful for words, and the Story Girl was elegant in her gorgeous new red dress. The walk home was the icing on the cake. A large, silvery moon hung low, and as it climbed higher, it created a star-spangled atmosphere that was almost fairylike. A little bubbling brook went with us part of the way, singing its song. Life seemed almost too good.

Life seemed especially good to Peter because Felicity allowed him to walk her home that night. When he asked her, she took his arm primly and marched off with him. How I envied Peter for his daring and carefree manner.

When I think back to those moments, they were full of pleasure. What a wonderful friendship we all had. We were simply friends and that was all that mattered. It was easy to see that although Peter wasn't part of our family now, he *might* be one day. And that was fun to think about.

How can I describe that night to you? The dark indigo sky was ablaze with millions of stars, and the wind blew through the fir trees making melodies that were heavenly. Perhaps it was the unearthly melodies made by the wind sweeping through the pines that made the Story Girl remember an old legend she had read in one of Aunt Olivia's books.

"It is called 'The Christmas Harp.' Would you like to hear it?" she asked.

"Oh, do tell it," Felix said. "It sounds like just what we need for our walk home tonight."

"It's about a shepherd who heard the Christmas angels sing. He was just a boy, and he loved music with all his heart and longed to be able to express the melody that was in his soul. But he could not. He had a harp, and he often tried to play it. But his clumsy fingers only made such discords that the other shepherds laughed at him and mocked him. They called him a madman because he would not give it up.

"When the other shepherds gathered around the fire and told tales to each other, he sat apart, holding his harp. The young shepherd enjoyed the dear silence that surrounded him and dreamed great thoughts about the heavens and the God who made them and the earth. Those thoughts were much sweeter than the rude stories and jokes the others told.

"And he never gave up the hope that someday he would be able to play his harp. Often he lifted his eyes heavenward and whispered a prayer that someday he could express musically all the thoughts in his heart about God. He promised that if he could ever play the harp, he would play to bring hope and encouragement to the dark, dreary world.

"On the first Christmas night, he was out with his fellow shepherds in the hills. It was chill and dark, and all the shepherds, except him, were gathered around the fire. As usual, he sat by himself with his harp on his knee and a great longing in his heart.

"Suddenly there came a marvelous light in the sky and over the hills. It was as if the darkness of the night had come alive with a burning flame. In the midst of the brilliant light, a great number of angels were singing a song that could only have come from Heaven itself.

"The harp the young shepherd held began to play softly by itself. It was playing the same music the angels were singing. All his secret longings were expressed in it. From that night forward, whenever he took the harp in his hands, it played the same music. He wandered all over the world carrying it. Wherever the sound of its music was heard, hatred was replaced with love, and discord with peace. No one who heard it could think an evil thought or feel hopeless or angry.

"When anyone heard the music, it was as though God entered into his soul and heart and became part of the person forever. Years went by, and the shepherd grew old, bent, and feeble. But he continued traveling with his harp, determined to carry the message of that

19

Christmas night to the ends of the earth. The old shepherd knew that the angel song had to be carried to all mankind, and he made that his ministry for life.

"At last his strength failed him, and he fell one night on a dark road in a wilderness where few came. As his spirit passed into Heaven, it seemed to him that a Shining One with wonderful, starry eyes stood by him. That One said to him, 'Lo, the music your harp has played all of these years has been the echo of the love and purity and beauty that dwells in your own soul. If you had ever opened the door of your heart to evil, selfishness, or wickedness, your harp would have stopped playing.

"'Now your life is ending. You have faithfully carried the message of God's redeeming love to mankind. No longer will you play an earthly harp, but you will join that great choir in Heaven. There you will receive God's "Faithful Servant Reward" and his "Well done!" You will live forever in that beautiful place as God's own child and heir.'"

We left the fir woods as the Story Girl finished her story. The King farm was just up the hill. A cozy dim light in the kitchen window told us that Aunt Janet was waiting up for us. She had no thought of going to bed before all of her "small fry," as she called us, were safely in for the night.

"Ma's waiting up for us," said Dan. "I'd have to laugh if she went to the door just as Felicity and

Peter were strutting up. I bet she'll be upset since it's almost midnight."

"Christmas will soon be over," said Cecily with a small sigh. "Hasn't it been a nice one? It's the first we've all spent together. Do you suppose we'll ever spend another one together as we are now?"

"Lots of 'em," said Dan cheerfully. "Why not?"

"Oh, I don't know," answered Cecily, her footsteps lagging somewhat. "Things just seem a little too pleasant to last."

"If Willy Fraser were walking Miss Cecily home, I don't think she'd be so low spirited," teased her brother.

Cecily tossed her head and chose to ignore him. There are some remarks a self-respecting young lady must ignore.

# New Year's Resolutions

*There's something very solemn about the idea of a New Year, isn't there? Just think about it—three hundred and sixty-five whole days and not a thing has happened in them yet.*

# Chapter Two

**E**ven though we didn't have a white Christmas, we had a snowy white New Year's. Between the two holidays, a heavy snowfall settled upon us that thrilled our hearts. It made the old orchard of delights even more delightful. It was so truly winter that it was hard to believe summer had ever dwelled there. No birds sang the music of the moon, and the path where the apple blossoms had fallen was heaped with huge drifts of snow. It was hard to imagine that spring would ever come to the orchard again.

But certainly, it was a place of wonder on a moonlit night. The snowy drifts shone like avenues of ivory and crystal, and the bare trees cast fairylike shadows upon them. The path we called Uncle Stephen's Walk seemed like a street of pearl in Heaven.

On New Year's Eve, we were all together in Uncle Alec's kitchen, where we spent most of our winter evenings. The Story Girl and Peter were there, of course, and Sara Ray's mother had allowed her to come up, as long as she promised to be home by eight sharp.

Cecily was glad to see her, but we boys were not too thrilled she had come. Since it was getting dark early these days, one of us always had to walk her down the hill to her home. We hated that because Sara Ray made a habit of acting like we were her *beaux* escorting her home.

We knew perfectly well that the next day in school she would tell one of her silly girlfriends that her "special friend" had walked her home. Of course, she made them swear never to tell the secret that so-and-so King saw her home. But we also knew her silly friends would make it the topic of the week, and we would be teased unmercifully.

Seeing a girl home because you *like* her is one thing, but seeing her home because your aunt *demands* it is a very different thing. We thought Sara Ray ought to have sense enough to understand that, but she never did. The simpering looks she would give Cecily were enough to make us sick. Of course it was lots of fun to tease the poor fellow who had to do the "honors," when he returned from his dutiful trek down the hill.

"Did you have fun, Felix?" or whoever it was. "Did you let her kiss you?" we'd jeer. It always ended in a great pillow fight that would continue until Aunt Janet stopped us and sent us off to bed.

But even though we pretended to be mad at each other, we loved the fun of being together.

On those winter evenings, a vivid rose sunset usually appeared behind the cold hills of pines, and the snowy fields glowed with a pink fairylike light. The drifts along the edges of the meadow looked as if a magician's wand had touched them with curls of whipped cream foam.

Sometimes we would creep out of bed and watch the dusk of the winter twilight turn to a deep navy blue as the moon rose. The stars would come out one by one, and the earth looked like a king's carpet for the new year to come.

"I'm so glad the snow came," the Story Girl said. "If it hadn't, the new year would have seemed just as dingy and worn out as the old. There's something very solemn about the idea of a new year, isn't there? Just think about it—three hundred and sixty-five whole days and not a thing has happened in them yet."

"I don't suppose anything very wonderful will happen in them," grumped Felix. Just then, Felix was feeling that life was all flat and stale. It was his turn to walk Sara Ray home.

"It makes me a little frightened to think of all that may happen in them," said Cecily. "My Sunday school teacher, Miss Marwood, says it is what we put into a year, not what we get out of it, that counts."

"I'm always glad to see a new year," said the Story Girl. "We ought to make some New Year's resolutions. It's a good thing to do."

"I can't think of any resolutions *I* need to make," said Felicity. She was perfectly satisfied with herself because she thought she was perfect. Any one of us could have told her differently.

"I could suggest a few to you," said Dan sarcastically.

"There are so many I'd like to make," Cecily said, "that I'm afraid I could never keep them all."

"Well, let's make a few, just for the fun of it, and see if we can keep them," I said. "I'll get some paper and ink and write them out. That will make them seem more solemn and binding."

"Then we can pin them up on our bedroom walls, where we'll see them every day," suggested the Story Girl, "and every time we break a resolution, we must put an X opposite it. That will show us what progress we are making, as well as make us ashamed if we have too many Xs."

"I think it's all nonsense," said Felicity. She joined our circle around the table, though she sat for a long time with a blank sheet before her.

"Let's take turns making resolutions," I said. "I'll lead off."

Remembering with shame some arguments I had had with Felicity, I wrote in my best handwriting, "I

28

will always try to keep my temper."

"You'd better," snipped Felicity. "No one else wants it."

I ignored her. It was Dan's turn next.

"I can't think of anything to start with," he said, gnawing his pen fiercely.

"You might make a resolution not to eat poisoned berries," suggested Felicity, referring to when Dan ate bad berries to spite Felicity.

"You'd better make one not to nag people ever-lastingly," I retorted. "Just because Dan ate some last year doesn't mean he will again."

"I will if she keeps reminding me about it," said Dan, shooting a hard look at his sister. "I'd rather be dead than put up with her jawing me all the time."

"Oh, don't quarrel the last night of the old year," begged Cecily.

"You might make a resolution not to quarrel anytime," suggested Sara Ray.

"No sir," said Dan emphatically. "There is no use making a resolution you can't keep. There are people in this family you've just *got* to quarrel with if you want to live. But I've thought of one. I won't do things to spite people." He wrote it down with a flourish.

"I will not eat any apples," wrote Felix.

"Why on earth do you want to give up eating apples?" asked Peter in surprise.

"Never mind," returned Felix.

"Apples make people *fat* you know," said Felicity in a sickeningly-sweet voice.

"It does seem like a funny kind of resolution," I said doubtfully. "I think our resolutions ought to be giving up wrong things or doing right ones."

"You make your resolutions to suit yourself, and I'll make mine to suit myself," Felix returned defiantly.

"I will never get drunk," wrote Peter, a bit ashamed.

"But you never have," said the Story Girl in astonishment.

"Well then, it will be all the easier to keep my resolution," argued Peter.

"That isn't fair," complained Dan.

"You let Peter alone," said Felicity severely. "It's a very good resolution and one everybody ought to make." She was so "holier than thou" we could hardly stand her.

"I will not be jealous," wrote the Story Girl.

"But are you?" I asked surprised.

The Story Girl turned red and nodded. "Of one thing," she confessed, "but I'm not going to tell what it is."

"I'm jealous sometimes, too," confessed Sara Ray, "so my first resolution will be this: I will try not to feel jealous when I hear the other girls in school describing all the sick spells they've had."

"Holy cow! You mean you *want* to be sick?" demanded Felix.

"It makes a person important," explained Sara Ray.

For the first time, I think, I began to understand Sara Ray. She was made to feel so badly all the time by her mother that she didn't feel she mattered to anyone. I guess she figured if she couldn't please her mother, she just wasn't important. Poor child! No wonder she cried all the time and made a lot of it when we walked her home. I made a silent resolution to be nicer to her and to try to make her feel important.

It was Cecily's turn next. "I am going to try to improve my mind by reading good books and listening to older people," wrote Cecily.

"It's your turn, Felicity," I said. Felicity tossed her beautiful blonde curls.

"I told you I wasn't going to make any resolutions. Go on yourself."

"I will always study my grammar lesson," I wrote.

"I hate grammar too," sighed Sara Ray.

"I won't get mad at Felicity, if I can help it," wrote Dan.

"I'm sure I never do anything to make you mad," exclaimed Felicity.

We all laughed at that, which *really* made her mad.

"I'll work all my arithmetic problems without any help," scribbled Felix, putting down another resolution.

"I won't play tic-tac-toe on the fly leaves of my hymnbook in church," wrote Peter.

"Mercy, did you ever do such a thing?" exclaimed Felicity in horror.

Peter nodded shamefacedly. "Yes—that Sunday Mr. Bailey preached. He was so long-winded and boring that I got awful tired, and anyway, he was talking about things I couldn't understand."

"Well, I hope if you ever do it again, you won't do it in *our* pew," said Felicity severely.

"I ain't gonna do it at all," said Peter. "I felt sorta mean all the rest of the day."

"I will not gossip," wrote Sara Ray with a satisfied smile.

"Oh, don't you think that's a little *too* strict?" asked Cecily. "Of course, it's not right to pass along *mean* gossip, but the harmless kind doesn't hurt. For instance, it's harmless gossip if I say Emmy MacPhail is going to get a new fur collar this winter. But if I say that I don't see how Emmy can afford a new fur collar when her father can't pay my father for the oats he got from him—that would be *mean* gossip. If I were you, Sara, I'd put *mean* gossip."

Sara consented to this new resolution.

"I will be polite to everybody," was my third resolution, which passed with no comment.

"I've thought of a resolution to make," cried Felicity. "Mr. Marwood said last Sunday that we should always try to think beautiful thoughts and then our lives will be beautiful. So I shall resolve that every time I see myself in the mirror, I'll think a beautiful thought."

"Can you only manage one a day?" asked Dan.

"I need something to inspire me," snipped Felicity, "and it will be easy to remember when I see my pretty face."

Dan looked at me, stuck his finger in his mouth, and made a noise as if he might throw up. She really did make us all sick with her conceited self. Felicity shot a look at her brother that could have killed.

"Peter, it's your turn," said Cecily.

"I will try," wrote Peter, "to say my prayers *every* night and not twice one night when I miss the night before."

"I suppose you never said your prayers until *we* got you to go to church," said Felicity, who had nothing whatever to do with Peter going to church. In fact, she had opposed it as she had said he was too ignorant and would embarrass us all.

"I said my prayers before I met any of you," said Peter, firmly. "My Aunt Jane taught me. Ma never had time since my father had run away and she had to work night and day doing people's washings."

"At least Peter says his prayers now," said the Story Girl, "and he's concerned enough about them to be honest about it. *My* next resolution is—I shall learn to cook."

"You'd better resolve not to make pudding of—" began Felicity. She stopped suddenly when Cecily gave her a poke in the ribs. Cecily had remembered the Story Girl's threat that she'd never tell another story if anyone reminded her of the pudding she had mistakenly made with sawdust instead of cornmeal. But we all knew what Felicity meant. And the look Sara Stanley gave Felicity made it clear that her mean remark was not appreciated.

"I will not cry because mother won't starch my aprons," wrote Sara Ray.

"Better resolve not to cry about anything," said Dan kindly.

Sara Ray shook her head sadly. "That would be too hard to keep. There are times when I just *have* to cry. It's a relief."

"Not to the ones who have to hear you," muttered Dan in a whisper to Cecily.

"Oh hush, Dan. Don't hurt her feelings," Cecily whispered, taking up for her friend. "Is it my turn again?" she spoke up. "Well, I resolve not to worry

34

because my hair isn't curly. But I'll never be able to keep from wishing it were."

"Why don't you curl it like you used to?" asked Dan.

"You know I gave that up when I prayed Peter would get well from the measles. It was something I promised God," she said sincerely.

Dan rolled his eyes and looked at me. "It's your go, Bev. Hurry it up," he said, anxious to get on with something else.

"I will try to keep my fingernails neat and clean. That's my fourth resolution. I don't think we should make more than four," I concluded.

"I'll try to think twice before I speak," said Felix.

"That will be an awful waste of time, but I guess it's a good idea since you are going to say exactly what you think all year," I answered.

"I'm going to stop with three resolutions," said Peter.

"That's what *I* call sensible," said Dan.

"It's a very easy resolution to keep, anyhow," commented Felix, referring back to his.

"I will try to like reading the Bible," wrote Sara Ray.

"You ought to like reading the Bible without trying to," exclaimed Felicity in her holier-than-thou voice.

"If you had to read seven chapters every time you were naughty, you wouldn't like it either," flashed Sara Ray.

"I'll try to obey mother *always*," wrote Sara Ray again, with a huge sigh, realizing how difficult that would be to keep. "And that's all I'm going to make."

"Felicity has made only one," said the Story Girl.

"I think it's better to make just one and keep it than to make a lot and break them," she said with her nose in the air again.

She had the last word on the subject, for it was time for Sara Ray to go home. Sara and Felix left, and we watched them go down the lane in the moonlight, Felix stalking along beside her as if he were going to a funeral. The silvery beauty of that romantic moment was thrown away on them. Felix was not happy.

As I remember it now, it was a most exquisite night and we went to bed with lofty thoughts in our heads, thinking that surely this year we could keep our resolutions. Time enough tomorrow to face the stark reality of how hard it would be to "think twice" or "believe only half" of what we heard. There was no doubt in any of our minds, however, that Felicity would think a beautiful thought each day. She had no trouble thinking she was beautiful.

# The Cousins' Scheme

*The wild January wind was shrieking
and howling outside, making noises like
a wounded animal. It was no day to be
outside in the storm that was whipping
across Prince Edward Island.*

# Chapter Three

All of us King cousins were sitting around the wood fire in Uncle Alec's kitchen. We were all there—Felix, Dan, Felicity, Cecily, and the Story Girl. Peter was there too, as usual. The wild January wind was shrieking and howling outside, making noises like a wounded animal. It was no day to be outside in the storm that was whipping across Prince Edward Island. So we were making the best of the stormy day by enjoying each other's company inside.

"I've thought of something exciting we can do this winter," I said.

We had been having a splendid game of blind-man's bluff, but stopped for a break and a drink of hot chocolate. "Tell us your idea, Bev," said the Story Girl, looking at me and giving a wink. I knew she thought this was the best time to launch the idea and scheme that she and I had been working on for a couple of weeks. She had insisted that I introduce the idea.

"You know how Felicity will never do anything I suggest?" she had said when we talked about it.

"And if she goes against it, Peter won't do it either—the ninny!"

There was not a doubt that Peter was in Felicity's pocket. That had been evident during our game of blindman's bluff when we noticed Peter was allowing himself to be caught on purpose, so he could catch Felicity. Whoever said, "Love is blind"? Peter could see through the five folds of woolen scarf with ease when he was trying to catch Felicity. What a goose!

Anyway, Sara had convinced me that since I was the oldest boy, I should suggest the scheme. And now was the time to do so, it seemed.

"What is it?" Felicity asked with interest.

"What would you think of us trying our hand at the newspaper business?" I asked in an offhand manner. I pretended to clean my fingernails with my pocketknife, as if their reaction were no big deal. "You know what I mean?" I continued. "We'd write all the articles, mostly about what we do ourselves. It could be a lot of fun."

Everyone looked a little blank and amazed, wondering where I had scraped up the idea. The Story Girl knew what she had to do, and she did it.

"What a silly idea," she sneered, giving a toss to her long brown curls. "As if we could do such a thing."

Felicity fired up just as we knew she would if the Story Girl seemed against it.

40

"*I* think it's a splendid idea," she said. "Why, we ought to be able to get up as good a newspaper as they have in town. Uncle Roger says the *Daily Enterprise* has gone to the dogs. All the news it prints is that some old woman went across the road to have tea with another old woman. I guess we could do better than that. You needn't think, Sara Stanley, that nobody but you can do something."

"I think it would be great fun," said Peter with decision. "My Aunt Jane helped edit a paper when she was at Queen's Academy. She said it was very amusing."

The Story Girl pretended to dislike the idea, frowning and shaking her head.

"Bev wants to be the editor," she said, "and I don't see how he can be with no experience. It would be a lot of hard work, if you ask me."

"Well, no one asked you, Miss Smarty," sniped Felicity. "You think you are the only one with ideas. And none of us are afraid of work, unless it's the Story Girl." Her eyes flashed with spirit. She and Sara Stanley were always competing with each other.

"I think it would be nice," said Cecily timidly, "and none of us have any more experience being editors than Bev. So that wouldn't matter."

"Will it be printed?" asked Dan.

"Oh no," I said. "We can't have it printed. We'll just have to write it out. We can buy school paper from the teacher."

"I don't think it will be much of a newspaper if it isn't printed," he retorted scornfully.

"It doesn't matter very much what *you* think," said Felicity spitefully to her brother.

"Thank you," said Dan sarcastically.

"Of course," said the Story Girl quickly, trying to avoid a quarrel, "if all the rest of you want it, I'll go along with it, too. Come to think of it, I think maybe it could be fun. We'll keep the copies, and when we become famous, they'll be quite valuable."

I hid my smile as I thought of how clever Sara and I had been to get all of them to agree. The Story Girl was always clever and usually had everything figured out, so she could get her way.

"Well, it's decided then," I said quickly. "The next thing we need to do is choose a name for the paper. That's a very important thing."

"How often are you going to publish it?" asked Felix.

"Once a month."

"I thought newspapers came out every day, or every week, at least," said Dan.

"We couldn't have one every week," I explained.

"It would be *too* much work."

"Well, that is an argument," admitted Dan. "The less work you can get along with the better, in my opinion. No Felicity, you needn't say it. I know what you're thinking, so save your breath to cool your soup. I agree with you that I never work if I can find anything else to do."

"Remember, it is harder to have no work to do than too much," said our wise Cecily.

"I don't believe *that*," argued Dan. "I'm like the man who said he wished the man who began work had stayed and finished it."

"Is it decided then that Bev will be the editor?" asked my brother, Felix.

"Of course," answered Felicity for everybody. She had a way of taking over for sure.

"I think it would be nice just to call the newspaper *Our Magazine*," Cecily said. "Then we'll all feel we have a part in it."

"*Our Magazine* it will be then," I said. "And as for having a share in it, you bet we all will. If I'm to be the editor, you must all be subeditors—each one in charge of a department."

"Oh, I couldn't," protested Cecily humbly.

"You must," I declared firmly. "Now what departments will we have? We must make it as much like a real newspaper as we can."

"Well, we ought to have an etiquette department, then," said Felicity. "The *Family Guide* magazine has one."

"Of course, we'll have one," I said. "Dan will edit it."

"Dan!" shrieked Felicity, who had hoped to be the etiquette editor herself.

"I guess I can write that column as well as the nitwit in the *Family Guide*," Dan answered defensively.

"But you can't have an etiquette department unless some questions are asked. What if no one asks any questions?" asked Cecily.

"Then you'll have to make some up," advised the Story Girl. "Uncle Roger says that must be what the *Family Guide* does. He says that no one could be as foolish as some of their questions are."

"We want you to edit the household department, Felicity," I said, noticing an angry flush on her face. She didn't like to be passed over. "No one can do that as well as you." The red face disappeared, and she looked pleased.

"Felix will edit the jokes and the Information Bureau. Cecily will be the fashion editor. And the Story Girl will attend to the gossip/personals column. They're very important. Anyone can contribute a personal, but the Story Girl is to see that there are some in every issue, even if she has to make them up—like Dan with the etiquette."

"Bev can do the scrapbook department and the editorials," said the Story Girl, seeing I was too modest to say it myself.

"Aren't we going to have a story page?" asked Peter.

"We will, if you'll be fiction and poetry editor," I said.

Peter was secretly put out, not wanting to do this. He had thought the Story Girl was a natural for it. But he didn't want to admit he couldn't do it in front of his beloved Felicity.

"All right," he said recklessly.

"We can put anything we like in the scrapbook department, but all the other columns must be original and state the names of the writers assigned to them. We'll all do our best. *Our Magazine* must be an outstanding paper."

"But you left out Sara Ray," said Cecily. "She'll feel awful bad if we don't give her a part in it."

I had forgotten Sara Ray. Nobody, except Cecily, ever remembered her unless she was present. But we decided to put her in as advertising manager. That sounded important, but meant very little.

"Well, it's settled," I said with a sigh of relief that it had been so easily decided. "We'll get the first issue out in January. And whatever else we do, we mustn't let Uncle Roger hear about it. He'll make terrible fun of it."

"I hope we can make a success of it," said Peter moodily. He was in a bad mood since he had been trapped into being the fiction editor.

"It will be a success if we are determined to succeed," I said. "Where there is a will, there is always a way."

"That's just what Ursula Townley said when her father locked her in her room on the night she was going to run away with Kenneth MacNair," said the Story Girl.

"Who were they?" I asked, sensing a story.

"Kenneth MacNair was a first cousin to one of the Awkward Man's grandfathers, and Ursula Townley was the most beautiful girl on the Island in her day."

"Who told you the story?" I asked, leaning forward with interest.

"You'll never believe," said the Story Girl mysteriously. "The Awkward Man read it to me right out of his brown notebook. I met him one day last week back in the maple woods. I was looking for wildflowers, and he was sitting by the creek, writing in his brown book. He hid it when he saw me and looked real silly. But after we had talked for a while, I came right out and asked him about it. I told him that the gossips said he wrote poetry in it. I asked him to tell me if it was true—I was dying to know. He said he wrote a little of everything in it. Then I begged him to read me something from the book, and he read me the story of Ursula and Kenneth."

"I don't see how you ever had the nerve," said Felicity, and even Cecily looked as if she thought the Story Girl had gone too far.

"Never mind that," cried Felix. "Tell us the story."

"I'll tell it just as the Awkward Man read it, but I can't put all of his nice poetical touches in. I can't remember them all, even though he read it twice for me." We settled back to listen as the logs on the fire burned brightly. The only sound was the crackling of the fire as she began the story.

# The Ball of Gray Yarn

*The bride held the hand of her bridegroom
lovingly, while in the other hand,
she held tightly to a treasured possession—
a ball of gray yarn.*

# Chapter Four

One day more than 100 years ago," began the Story Girl, "Ursula Townley was waiting for Kenneth MacNair in a wood. An October wind was making the leaves dance on the ground like pixie people.

"Prince Edward Island wasn't the same 100 years ago as it is today," continued Sara Stanley. "There weren't many little towns, and they were far apart. Old Hugh Townley boasted that he knew every man, woman, and child on the Island. And he did.

"Old Hugh was an important man then. Not only was he rich, but he was well-known for his generous ways. He was also extremely proud of his daughter, who was the most beautiful girl on the Island. She had so many lovers that all the other girls hated her. But she only had eyes for one dark-eyed young sea captain, Kenneth MacNair.

"As far as Old Hugh was concerned, the sea captain was the last person he would have chosen for his daughter. He had forbidden her to invite him to their home. The reason for the father's furious

51

dislike really had nothing to do with Kenneth himself. Old Hugh hated Kenneth MacNair because the young man's father had beaten him in a political election long before. Hugh had never forgiven the son for the father's victory, and the feud had carried on between the families for thirty years. So, Ursula had to sneak out to meet Kenneth if she wanted to see him.

"On a Sunday, Kenneth's brother had secretly slipped a letter from his brother to Ursula asking her to meet Kenneth the next day.

"When Ursula's suspicious father and watchful stepmother thought she was spinning wool in the barn loft, she slipped away to meet Kenneth in the beech woods."

"It was very wrong of her to deceive her parents," said Felicity primly.

The Story Girl agreed, but said, "I'm not telling about what Ursula Townley *ought* to have done. I'm only telling you what she *did* do. If you don't want to hear it, you needn't listen, Felicity. There wouldn't be many stories to tell if people never did anything they shouldn't do."

Felicity sniffed, but continued listening. She couldn't bear the thought of not hearing the rest of the story.

"When Kenneth and Ursula met, it was as one might expect from two lovers who had not had a kiss for three months. After their kiss Ursula said, 'Oh Kenneth, I can't stay long. You said in your letter that you had something important to say to me. What is it?'

"'My news is this, Ursula. Next Saturday morning, my vessel, *The Fair Lady*, and I must sail from the Charlottetown harbor for Brazil. I won't return until next May.'

"'Kenneth!' cried Ursula. She turned pale and burst into tears.

"'Why sweetheart! I want to take you with me,' laughed Kenneth. 'We'll spend our honeymoon on the high seas. I know an old preacher who can marry us aboard the ship.'

"'You want me to run away with you, Kenneth? My father will never—'

"'Ursula dear, he won't know 'til we are far away. Your father will never forgive me because of what my father did. Be courageous.'

"'What is your plan?' asked Ursula breathlessly.

"'Are you invited to the party next week at the Springs' house?'

"'Yes,' she nodded.

"'Good. I'm not, but I'll be there in the fir trees behind the house. I'll have two horses. In the middle of the party, you must steal out to meet me. It's only fifteen miles from Charlottetown to our ship. The old minister will be waiting there to marry us. By the time anyone knows we're gone, we will be out to sea.'

"'And if I'm not there—then what?'

"'Then I will sadly sail for South America, my love, and it will be a long time before we see each other again.'

"Perhaps Kenneth hadn't meant it, but his answer was enough to convince Ursula. She decided to run away with him.

"When Friday night came, Ursula dressed for the party. Then she looked at herself in the mirror and smiled happily. Yes, Felicity, she was a vain, little girl—like someone else I know.

"But Ursula had good reason to be proud of her looks," continued Sara. "She was wearing a sea green dress that had been brought from England the year before. She had only worn it one other time. It was a fine, rustling silk that set off her auburn hair and gleaming brown eyes. Those eyes held the secret that she was to be a bride that very night. The thought of it touched her cheeks with crimson, making her even more beautiful than usual.

"As Ursula turned from admiring herself in the mirror, she heard her father's voice below, loud and angry. Growing very pale, she ran out into the hall. Her father was coming up the stairs, his face red with fury. At the door in the hall below her stood a homely neighbor boy named Malcolm Ramsey. He had always had a crush on the beautiful Ursula.

"'Ursula, this scoundrel tells me you met up with that dog, Kenneth MacNair, in the woods this week. Tell me that he's a liar,' bellowed Old Hugh.

"Ursula was not a coward, nor was she a liar. 'Malcolm may be a sneak and a talebearer, but he tells the truth. I did meet Kenneth last Tuesday,' she admitted.

"'Then get back into your room and take off that finery,' Old Hugh roared. 'You'll not go to any more parties if I can't trust you. You'll stay in your room 'til I choose to let you out. And take this knitting with you. You can keep yourself amused with it all evening,' he said in anger, tossing her a ball of gray knitting wool.

"The ball of wool rolled into her room, and Ursula followed it with her head high in the air. Slamming the door, she flung herself down on her bed for a good cry.

"Then she began to pace up and down in her room. *Oh, what's to be done? Kenneth will think I decided not to come. He will leave, and I will become an old maid. I will go mad,* she thought.

"For the rest of the afternoon, she cried and fumed. Suddenly she heard hoof beats on the lane leading to the house. Looking out, she saw Andrew

Kine, one of her father's friends. He was dismounting and coming to the door. She heard the servant answer the door and let him in to see Old Hugh. Listening through the stovepipe, she heard Andrew say that he was going to the party at the Springs' later that night.

"Suddenly she had an idea. Sitting down at her desk, she scrawled a note to Kenneth, telling him what had happened. Then she unwound the ball of gray yarn a bit and pinned the note inside. Winding the wool back around and around, she concealed the note. Pinning it with a straight pin, so it would not unravel, she quietly raised her window and waited until she heard Andrew leaving.

"It was just getting dark as Andrew said his good-byes. Fortunately Old Hugh did not go out the door with him. As Andrew untied his horse, Ursula threw the ball of yarn with such good aim that it hit him right on the head, just as she had meant it to do. Andrew looked up at her window.

"She leaned out and put her finger on her lips, warning him to be quiet. Then she pointed to the ball and made a motion for him to take it and go. He looked at her quite puzzled, but jamming it into his pocket, he jumped into the saddle and took off.

"*So far so good*, thought Ursula. *But will he think to unwind the ball and read the note?* she wondered. *And even if he does, will he deliver it to Kenneth, knowing my father is so opposed?*

"The evening dragged by. It seemed to Ursula that time had never passed so slowly. She could not rest or sleep. It was almost midnight when she heard the patter of a handful of gravel on her windowpane. Quietly she leaned out. Standing below in the darkness was her lover, Kenneth MacNair.

"'Oh, Kenneth, did you get my note?' she whispered. 'And is it safe for you to be here?'

"'Safe enough. Your father is in bed. I've waited for two hours down the road for his light to go out and an extra half-hour to be certain he's asleep. I have the horses. Are you ready to go?'

"'Easier said than done,' said Ursula. 'I'm locked in, my love. You'll have to get the ladder from behind the barn.'

"A few minutes later, Miss Ursula, hooded and cloaked, climbed silently down the ladder, and she and Kenneth were dashing down the road.

"'We've a long ride ahead, Ursula,' said Kenneth. 'It's fifteen miles further from here than it would have been from the Springs' house.'

"'It's all right. I'd ride to the ends of the earth with you, Kenneth MacNair,' she said smiling.

"The next morning, as a red sun rose over the Charlottetown harbor, the newlyweds stood on the deck of *The Fair Lady* as it sailed for South America. The bride held the hand of her bridegroom lovingly, while in the other hand, she held tightly to a treasured possession—a ball of gray yarn."

"I like that kind of story," said Dan as she ended the tale. "Nobody goes and dies in it."

"It must be rather romantic to be run away with," remarked Cecily wistfully.

"You get those silly notions out of your head, Cecily King," said Felicity severely.

# Hot Off the Press

Poor Felicity never caught on that we had just been pretending to be against starting the paper so she wouldn't be opposed to the idea, like she usually was to everything we suggested. We were delighted to have put one over on her.

# *Chapter Five*

T he first edition of *Our Magazine* was ready on January 30. That evening in Aunt Janet's kitchen, we took turns reading from it and patting ourselves on the back for a job well done. For the most part, we were very proud of it. Dan still continued to scoff at the idea of a paper that wasn't really printed, but he stayed around for the first reading. We took turns reading while the others ate apples. That is, all of us were eating apples except Felix. He did not dare since he had made a resolution not to eat them. The Story Girl, the first reader, read the editorial to us. It went like this:

This first edition of the newspaper, *Our Magazine*, is proudly presented. All the editors of the various departments have done their very best, and we know you'll find it full of information and amusement.

The cover has been designed by Mr. Blair Stanley, a famous European artist. It was sent to us from Paris at the request of his daughter, Sara Stanley, one of our contributing editors. Mr. Peter Craig, our literary editor, has given us a touching love story. His article follows. *(Peter whispered, "I ain't never been called a mister before.")*

## The Story of an Elopement from Church

By Peter Craig

This is a true story. It happened in Markdale to one of my relatives. My mother's uncle wanted to marry Miss Jemima Parr. Jemima Parr's father wanted her to marry a rich man, so he told my relative, Thomas Taylor, not to come near their house or he'd set the dogs on him. Thomas was nearly crazy for the love of Jemima Parr, and she wanted to marry him, too.

Well, he was a pretty smart young man. He waited 'til there was a preaching day in Markdale. He knew all of Jemima's family would be at church, since her father was an elder. He and Jemima had it all worked out between them.

As soon as they began to sing the last hymn, Thomas Taylor left the church. When the prayer was over, Jemima walked out quickly, too. Before the family knew what was happening, Thomas and Jemima had run off together in her father's sleigh.

Everyone said they lived happily ever after. My relative Thomas Taylor lived to be a very old man.

Next the Story Girl read Cecily's article:

## My Most Exciting Adventure

By Cecily King

My most exciting adventure happened a year ago last November. I was nearly frightened to death. Dan says he wouldn't of been a skeered and Felicity says she would of known what it was, but it's easy to talk.

It happened one night when I went down to see Kitty Marr. I thought my Aunt Olivia was visiting there, and I could come home with her. She wasn't, so I had to come home alone, because Kitty would only come part of the way with me. She said it wasn't because she was afraid of the ghost dog that people said haunted the bridge in Uncle James' hollow. But I knew Kitty wasn't telling the truth. I had heard the story about the ghost dog, but I pretended not to be afraid when I started across the bridge.

I knew there was no such thing as ghosts, and I started bravely across. I was saying a Scripture verse over and over and also the Golden Rule text for the Sunday school lesson that Sunday. But my heart was beating real hard.

Just as I got to the middle of the bridge, I saw something big and black coming right at me. It was about the size of a big Newfoundland dog. It kept jumping in front of me whichever way I tried to go. I was too skeered to run back, and I couldn't get past it. Just as I thought I could make it around the thing, it jumped right on top of me, and I felt its claws. I screamed and screamed and fell down. Then I lay there real quiet, not daring to move, and the thing was quiet, too.

I don't know what would have happened to me if Amos Cowan hadn't come along that very minute with a lantern. When I saw his light, I jumped up. And what do you think—that thing I thought was a big black dog was Amos Cowan's big black umbrella that had gotten away from him in the wind.

I don't know what he was doing with an open umbrella because it wasn't raining. But I didn't ask him.

Amos asked if I wanted to have him take me home. You bet your life I did. I was very thankful for him to walk me the rest of the way home, even if it did seem kind of crazy that he had that umbrella open when it wasn't even raining.

Felicity read Cecily's "Fashion Notes," with the boys pretending to model each item she read.

### Fashion Notes

By Cecily King
our fashion editor

Knitted mufflers are much more stylish than crocheted ones this winter. It is nice to have one the same color as your cap. Red mittens with a black diamond pattern are much the rage this year. Em Frewen's grandma knits hers for her. She can knit the double diamond pattern and Em puts on such airs about it. Personally, I think the single diamond pattern is in better taste.

The new winter hats at Markdale are very pretty. It is so exciting to pick a hat. Boys can't have that fun. Their hats are so much alike and boring. *(Peter's remark in a loud whisper: "Your hat is so pretty, Dan!")*

Poor Felicity never caught on that we had just been pretending to be against starting the paper so she wouldn't be opposed to the idea, like she usually was to everything we suggested. We were delighted to have put one over on her.

What harmless, happy fooling it all was! How we laughed as we read and listened and ate apples. *Our Magazine* never made much of a stir in the world, but we sure had fun writing it all year.

# Great-Aunt Eliza's Visit

*This hilarity went on so long we were
nearly lying on the floor trying to keep
our laughter down. I don't know what
we would have done had Felicity
not appeared at the doorway with a
white face and panic-stricken eyes.*

# Chapter Six

t was a diamond winter day in February—clear, cold, hard, and brilliant. The sharp blue sky shone, the white fields and hills glittered. Icicles hung like sparkling jewels around the edges of Uncle Alec's roof. We kids were all excited for it was Saturday, and we were left alone to keep house. Our grown-ups had gone into Charlottetown for the day. They left us lots of rules and instructions as usual. Some of these we remembered, and some we forgot. But with Felicity in command, none of us dared stray too far.

We laid out our plans carefully. We would get all of our work done in the morning and have the whole glorious afternoon for sledding. Before lunch we would have a taffy-pull. We did manage to get to the candy making, but before we could get it pulled to our satisfaction, Felicity glanced out the window and groaned.

"Oh dear! Here comes Great-Aunt Eliza. Can you beat it? And we were having such fun."

We all looked out to see a tall, gray-haired lady coming up the walk to the front door. She looked around with the puzzled look of a stranger. We had been expecting Aunt Eliza for weeks, but we weren't quite sure when she would arrive. She had been visiting other relatives in Markdale. Aunt Janet said she would likely show up to "surprise" us—and here she was.

None of us had really been looking forward to her coming. Although we had never met her, we knew she was very deaf and not particularly fond of children.

"Whew!" whistled Dan, looking out the window. "We're in for it. She's deaf as a post, and we'll have to shout to make her hear at all."

"Look! She can't get to the front door," said Felicity. "I told you, Dan. You should have shoveled the snow away from the front door this morning. Cecily, pick up those pots and the candy mess. Hide the boots, Felix. She's coming around to the back door. Shut the cupboard door, Peter. Sara, straighten up the sofa. She's awful particular and Ma says her house is as neat as a pin."

To be fair, Felicity was flying around herself while she was issuing orders. It was amazing how much was accomplished putting the house in order during the two minutes Great-Aunt Eliza spent going around to the back of the house.

"Fortunately the sitting room is tidy and there's plenty in the pantry," said Felicity.

There was no more conversation then as Great-Aunt Eliza gave a sharp rap on the window of the kitchen door. Felicity opened it.

"Why how do you do, Aunt Eliza?" she said loudly.

A slightly puzzled look appeared on Aunt Eliza's face. Felicity thought she hadn't heard her.

"How do you do, Aunt Eliza?" she repeated at the top of her voice. "Come in. We're glad to see you. We've been looking for you for ever so long."

"Are your father and mother at home?" asked Aunt Eliza slowly.

"No, they went to town today. But they'll be home this evening."

"I'm sorry they're away," said Aunt Eliza, coming in. "I can only stay a few hours."

"Oh, that's too bad," shouted poor Felicity, giving us angry looks as if to demand we help her out.

"Well, take off your things and stay for tea at least," begged Felicity. Her vocal chords were straining, and she was getting hoarse.

"Yes, I think I'll do that. I want to get acquainted with my—my nephews and nieces," she said with a rather pleasant glance at all of us. I could have almost sworn there was a twinkle in her eye. But no, that wasn't possible. "Won't you introduce yourselves please?"

Felicity shouted our names and Great-Aunt Eliza shook hands all around. She was very tall and dignified and grim. I figured I was mistaken about a twinkle in her eye. There was no smile about her. Felicity and Cecily took her to the sitting room and then returned to the kitchen to make the tea.

"Well, what do you think of dear Aunt Eliza?" asked Dan.

"*Sssh*," warned Cecily, with a glance at the half-open door.

"Piffle! She can't hear us. There ought to be a law against anyone being as deaf as that."

"She's not so old looking as I expected," said Felix. "If her hair wasn't so white, she wouldn't look much older than Aunt Janet."

"You don't have to be very old to be a great-aunt," said Cecily. "I expect it was burying so many husbands that turned her hair white. She doesn't seem as old as I expected, though."

"She's dressed more stylishly than I expected," said Felicity. "I thought she'd be real old-fashioned, but her clothes aren't too bad. I'm going to be very nice to her because she's rich," she said with her usual conceited logic. "But how are we going to entertain her?"

"What does the *Family Guide* say about entertaining your rich, old aunt?" said Dan. He seemed delighted to see Felicity on the hot seat.

"Be quiet, Dan. Sara, can you run over to your house and get some stale bread? I heard Father say that fresh bread gives her indigestion. I'll make some cinnamon toast to go with the tea."

"I'll make the toast," volunteered Sara. "I can do that real well."

"No, it wouldn't do to trust you," said Felicity in her uppity way. "I'll make the toast if you'll go get some old bread. You might make some bad mistake, and then she'd tell it all over town. I hear she's an awful gossip, so we must watch our step.

"I've heard she hates cats—so be sure you lock up Paddy," Felicity went on.

"Do you think it would be all right for me to ask her for her name to put on my quilt square?" asked Cecily. "I believe I will. She looks a lot friendlier than I expected. She'll probably choose the five-cent section. I'm sure she's economical."

"Well, I'm going to see about getting the tea," said Felicity. "The rest of you will have to entertain her. Go get the photo album. Dan, you know everybody in it. You do it."

"Not on your life," said Dan. "That's a girl's job. Wouldn't I look sweet cozied up to her yelling

73

about Cousin Sarah's twins. Cecily or the Story Girl can do it."

"Not me," said the Story Girl quickly. "I don't know all your relatives on your mother's side."

"I guess I'll have to do it," grumped Cecily. "Let's go in. She'll think we have awful manners if we leave her any longer."

We all filed in reluctantly. Great-Aunt Eliza was toasting her toes at the fire—clad, we noticed, in very smart and shapely shoes. Cecily did her brave best, but she couldn't shout as loud as Felicity. Half the time it seemed our great-aunt didn't even hear her. Or at least she acted like she didn't know the cousins and family whom Cecily pointed out so patiently. Every once in a while, she smiled. Somehow I didn't like her smile. It seemed sneaky and very un-great-auntish.

The Story Girl was all out of sorts, probably because she couldn't charm our deaf aunt with her storytelling wit and charm. Finally, Dan came to our rescue by making up funny things to say about every picture that Cecily explained. It was all we could do to smother our laughter. Dan was saying it just loud enough for us to hear, knowing our deaf auntie couldn't hear any of the outrageous things he was saying. This is how it went.

Cecily, shouting: "This is Mr. Joseph Elliott of Markdale, a second cousin of mother's."

Dan: "Don't brag about him, Sis. He's been married four times. Don't you think that's often enough, Auntie?"

Cecily, giving Dan a hard look: "This is a nephew of Mr. Ambrose Marr's. He lives out West and teaches school."

Dan: "Yes, and Uncle Roger says he doesn't have enough sense to come in out of the rain."

This hilarity went on so long that we were nearly lying on the floor trying to keep our laughter down. I don't know what we would have done had Felicity not appeared at the doorway with a white face and panic-stricken eyes.

"Cecily, come here for a moment please," she said in a tight, nervous voice.

"What's the matter, Felicity?" we heard her ask.

"Matter!" screamed Felicity in a loud whisper. "Story Girl must have let Paddy out when she went to get the bread. One of you left a plate of molasses on the pantry table, and Paddy got into it and what do you think? He went into the spare room and walked all over Aunt Eliza's things on the bed. You can see his tracks all over her things. What on earth can we do?"

Aunt Eliza was still looking at the picture album, but she must have thought something was funny because she was smiling widely.

"Well, let's take a little clean water and a soft bit of cotton and see if we can't clean the molasses off," said our wise little Cecily.

"We can try, but I wish the Story Girl would keep her cat at home," grumbled Felicity.

Apparently it worked, because the girls never mentioned the incident to Aunt Eliza. Tea was served and was a great success. There was some discussion behind the kitchen door about who would say the prayer for the tea. It was decided to ask Aunt Eliza, and she did without any hesitation. The cinnamon toasts were wonderful, and all of us relaxed as we enjoyed it. None of us were saying much until after the tea when the Story Girl asked us if we knew the present governor's wife.

"She is a friend of Father's, but we've never met her. Her name is Agnes Clark. When Father was a young man, he was very much in love with her and she with him," replied Felicity.

"Who ever told you that?" exclaimed Dan.

"Aunt Olivia. And I've heard Ma teasing Father about it, too. Of course, it was before Father got acquainted with Mother," answered Felicity.

"Why didn't your father marry her?" asked the Story Girl.

"I guess she fell out of love with him. She was pretty fickle. Aunt Olivia said Father felt awful about it for a while, but he got over it when he met Ma. Ma was twice as good-looking as Agnes Clark. Aunt Olivia says that Agnes had a lot of freckles. But she and Father were good friends. Just think—if she had married Father, we would be the governor's children."

"But she wouldn't have been the wife of the governor then," said Dan.

"I guess it's just as good being the wife of Father," said Cecily loyally.

"You might think so if you saw the governor," chuckled Dan.

"You've been listening to Uncle Roger," said Cecily. "Uncle Roger just makes fun of him because he's on the opposite side of politics. The governor isn't really so ugly. I saw him at the Markdale picnic two years ago. He's very fat and bald, but I've seen worse looking."

"I'm afraid your seat is too near the stove, Aunt Eliza," shouted Felicity.

Indeed our guest had a very red face and was making a strange strangled noise—almost like laughter. We looked at her, and somehow we didn't talk much after that. Soon she said she had to go. Felicity politely urged her to stay, but we all were much relieved when she left.

Afterward, we sat around the fire discussing her visit. "There is something rather odd about her," said the Story Girl.

"Oh well, never mind," said Cecily. "She's gone now, and that's the last of it."

But it wasn't the last of it—not by a long shot. When our grown-ups returned, the first words Aunt Janet said were, "And so you had the governor's wife to tea."

We all stared at her. "There was a lady here to tea," said Felicity miserably. "We thought she was Great-Aunt Eliza and—"

"Nonsense! Aunt Eliza was in town today. She had tea with us at Aunt Louisa's. But we met Governor Lesly's wife, Agnes Clark, on her way back to Charlottetown. She told us she was here for tea. Seems she was visiting a friend in Carlisle and thought she'd just drop in on us."

"Oh no!" groaned Cecily. "We thought she acted strangely. We knew you said Aunt Eliza was deaf, so we were all shouting at her—and Dan—"

"What did Dan do?" asked Aunt Janet.

"He thought she couldn't hear, so he made up all kinds of stories when I was trying to show her the family photo album," answered Cecily.

"Can't I trust any of you to act civilized," said Aunt Janet sternly. "Oh my, what she must think of us."

"I think it was real mean of her to pretend to be deaf," said Felicity, almost on the verge of tears.

"That's Agnes Clark for you," chuckled Father. "What a splendid time she must have had this afternoon. I bet she really enjoyed herself."

The next day, we learned that she had indeed enjoyed herself when this letter came from her:

*Dear Cecily and all the rest of you,*

*I want to ask you to forgive me for pretending to be your Aunt Eliza. When you thought I was, I couldn't resist having a little fun. If you will forgive me for it, I will forgive you for the things you said about the governor, and we will be good friends. He is really a nice man, though he may not be too handsome.*

*I had a splendid time at your place, and I envy your Aunt Eliza who has such nice nephews and nieces. You were all so kind to me. But I didn't dare be nice to you, or I would have given it away that I wasn't Aunt Eliza. I'll make it all up to you if you will come to see me at the governor's palace the next time you come to town. I'm sorry I didn't get to see Paddy, for I do love pussycats. And Cecily, the governor wants you to put his name on your quilt in the ten-cent section. I'm enclosing the money.*

*Tell Dan that his comments made the photo time a real treat. That boy has a great sense of humor. I'll look forward to seeing all of you soon. Do send me your recipe for the cinnamon toast, Felicity. It was most unusual.*

*Yours most cordially,*
*Agnes Clark Lesly*

"Why Felicity! What a triumph to have the governor's wife ask for your recipe. What did you use to make the cinnamon toast so good?" asked Aunt Janet.

"I rolled them in the special sugar in the pantry," Felicity said. "You know, the one with the yellow label."

Aunt Janet stared at her daughter, then she broke into laughter.

"Felicity King, that was tooth powder! When she was here last winter, Cousin Myra broke the bottle her tooth powder was in. I gave her that old can, and she forgot to take it when she left."

Felicity's pride in her cooking crumbled, and she flushed red. I thought she was going to cry until Peter spoke up.

"I didn't think it was bad at all, Felicity. And if the governor's wife liked the toast, it must have been all right," he soothed.

"Sure, Sis. Be sure to send her the recipe," jeered Dan. "She will probably tell the whole town about it."

Felicity ran out of the room, and we heard the angry slam of her door. For sure, the governor's wife never got that recipe, even though we all had a wonderful tea at the governor's palace some weeks later. Felicity finally had come down off her high horse about her cooking. I know the Story Girl was happy about that.

# We Visit Cousin Mattie

*We had expected a good dinner at Cousin Mattie's, and we got one. They were very kind to us, although I understood why Dan objected to them. When we left, they patted us all on the head, told us whom we looked like, and gave us peppermint lozenges—like we were five years old.*

# Chapter Seven

One Saturday in March, we decided that we would walk over to Baywater and have a visit with our Cousin Mattie. Baywater was only six miles away, but there was a shortcut across the hills and fields. We didn't look forward to our visit with any great delight, however. Nobody was ever at Cousin Mattie's except some older women relatives.

We decided that we might as well go and get it over with.

"Anyhow we'll have a splendiferous dinner," said Dan. "Cousin Mattie is a great cook and there is nothing stingy about her."

"You're always thinking of your stomach," said Felicity pleasantly, for a change.

"Well, you know I couldn't get along very well without it, darling," responded Dan, who, since New Year's, had adopted a new way of dealing with his sister, and it really got her goat. Felicity always got furious when he called her darling or sweetheart because she knew he was being sarcastic.

Uncle Alec was doubtful about our going that day. He looked out at the gray earth and gray air and gray sky and said that a storm was brewing. But Cousin Mattie had been sent word that we were coming, and she didn't like to be disappointed. He let us go, warning us to stay with Cousin Mattie all night if the storm came up while we were there.

We enjoyed our walk. What did it matter to us if the world was gray and wintry? We walked the golden road and carried springtime in our hearts. We joked our way along with laughter and listened to the Story Girl's tales. Even Felix enjoyed it, although he had been appointed to write up the visit for *Our Magazine* and was weighed down by the responsibility of it all.

The walking was easy for everything was frozen. The way we were going took us near the place where old Peg Bowen lived. She was a fierce old woman, but we had gotten to know her pretty well. We still hoped we wouldn't meet up with her though. We were never quite comfortable around her.

The woods were full of that brooding stillness that often comes before a storm. The wind was starting to pick up with a low wailing cry. None of us were sorry when we got through the woods and found ourselves looking down over the hill into the snug village of Baywater.

"There's Cousin Mattie's house—that big white one at the turn of the road," said the Story Girl. "I hope she has that dinner ready, Dan. I am as hungry as a wolf after our walk."

"I wish Cousin Mattie's husband were still alive," said Dan. "He was an awfully nice old man. He always had his pockets full of nuts and apples. I used to like going there better when he was alive. Too many old women don't suit me."

"Oh Dan, Cousin Mattie and her sisters-in-law are just as nice and kind as they can be," said Cecily.

"Oh, they're kind enough, but they never seem to see that a fellow gets over being five years old— if he only lives long enough," answered Dan.

We had expected a good dinner at Cousin Mattie's, and we got one. They were very kind to us, although I understood why Dan objected to them. When we left, they patted us all on the head, told us whom we looked like, and gave us peppermint lozenges—like we were five years old. All in all, it wasn't as bad as we had thought it would be. Cousin Mattie was a very nice cousin for an old lady, and we had a good time.

# Lost in the Blizzard

*In my heart, I didn't believe that we would ever get through alive. It was almost pitch dark now, and the snow grew deeper with each step. We were chilled to the bone. I thought about how nice it would be to lie down and rest, but I remembered hearing that lying down was fatal in a snowstorm.*

# Chapter Eight

We left Cousin Mattie's early, for it still looked like a storm was brewing. We had intended to go home a different way that would lead us away from old Peg Bowen's house, and we thought we would be home before it started to storm. Before we reached the top of the hill, however, a fine driving snow began to fall. It would have been wiser to turn back even then. But we had already come a mile and thought we would have ample time to reach home before it became really bad.

We were sadly mistaken. By the time we had gone another half-mile, we were in the midst of a blinding snowstorm. We were too far from Cousin Mattie's to go back, so we decided to struggle on. We were growing more frightened with each step. We could hardly face the stinging snow, and we couldn't see ten feet in front of us. It had turned very cold with the wind whirling around us, and night was coming quickly.

The narrow path we were trying to follow soon disappeared, and we stumbled blindly on, holding on to each other and trying to see through the furious whirl of snow. It had come upon us so suddenly, before we even realized it. Peter was leading because he knew the best path. But now, he stopped.

"I can't see the road any longer!" he shouted. "I don't know where we are."

We all stopped and huddled together in a miserable little group. Fear filled our hearts. It seemed like it had been ages since we had been snug, safe, and warm at Cousin Mattie's. Cecily began to cry because of the cold. Dan, in spite of her protests, took off his overcoat and made her put it on.

"We can't stay here," he said. "We'll all freeze to death if we do. Come on—we have to keep moving. The snow ain't so deep yet. Take one of my hands, Sis. We must all stay together. Come on now."

"It won't be very pleasant to freeze to death—but if we get through alive, think of the story we'll have to tell," said the Story Girl with chattering teeth.

In my heart, I didn't believe that we would ever get through alive. It was almost pitch dark now, and the snow grew deeper with each step. We were chilled to the bone. I thought about how nice it would be to lie down and rest, but I remembered hearing that lying down was fatal in a snowstorm.

So I stumbled on with the others. It was wonderful how the girls kept up—even Cecily. It occurred to me to be thankful that Sara Ray was not with us.

We were totally lost now. Darkness and horror were all around us. Suddenly, Felicity fell. We dragged her up, but she declared that she could not go on— she was done for.

"Have you any idea where we are?" shouted Dan to Peter.

"No! The wind is blowing every which way. I don't have any idea which way to go."

Home! Would we ever see it again? We tried to urge Felicity on, but she only repeated drowsily that she must lie down and rest. Cecily, too, was tired. The Story Girl still stood staunchly and tried to struggle on even though she was numb with cold. Her words were not understandable. I got a wild idea in my mind that we should dig a hole in the snow and all huddle in it. I had read that people saved their lives by doing that.

Suddenly Felix gave a shout. "I see a light," he cried.

"Where?" We all looked, but could see nothing.

"I don't see it now, but I saw it a moment ago," shouted Felix. "I'm sure I did. Come on—over in this direction."

Inspired with fresh hope, we hurried after him. Soon we all saw the light—and never was it more welcome. A few more steps, and we came into the shelter of the woodland. It was then that we knew where we were.

"That's Peg Bowen's house," exclaimed Peter, stopping short in dismay.

"I don't care whose house it is," declared Dan. "We've got to get to it."

"I suppose so," said Peter. "We can't freeze to death, even if she is crazy."

"For goodness sake! Don't say anything about that so close to her house," gasped Felicity. "I'll be thankful to get in anywhere."

We reached the house, climbed the flight of steps that led to a second-story door on which Dan knocked. The door opened promptly and there stood Peg Bowen right before us. She had on her usual ragbag costume that she always wore.

Behind her was a dim room lit by one small candle. An old Waterloo stove was covering the gloom with red whirls of light. It seemed very warm and cozy, like a retreat to us.

"Goodness gracious! Where'd y'all come from?" exclaimed Peg. "Did they turn ya out?"

"We were over at Baywater and got lost in the storm on our way home," explained Dan. "We didn't know where we were until we saw your light. I guess we will have to stay here until the storm is over—if you don't mind."

"And if it won't inconvenience you," said Cecily timidly.

"Oh, it's no inconvenience to speak of. Come on in. Well, y'all do have some snow on you. Let me get a broom. You boys stomp your feet real good and shake your coats. You girls, gimme your things and I'll hang 'em up. Guess y'all are almost froze to death. Well, get up close to the stove."

Peg bustled away to gather up an odd assortment of chairs. Most of them had backs and rungs missing. In a few minutes, we were in a circle around her roaring stove, getting dried and thawed out. In our wildest flights of imagination, we had never pictured ourselves as guests at Peg Bowen's fireplace. Yet there we were. And Peg was, at that very moment, brewing some ginger tea for Cecily, who was still shivering, long after the rest of us had warmed up. Poor Cecily drank that scalding tea, too fearful of Peg to do otherwise.

"That will soon fix your shivers," said our hostess. "And now I'll get you all some tea."

"Oh, please don't trouble yourself," said the Story Girl.

"Ain't any trouble at all," said Peg briskly.

Then with one of the sudden changes to fierceness that made her such a terrifying person, she said, "Did y'all think my vittles ain't clean?"

We didn't usually call food "vittles," but we knew what she meant.

"Oh, no, no!" cried Felicity quickly. "None of us would ever think that. Sara only meant that she didn't want you to go to any trouble on our account."

"It ain't any bother," said Peg. "I'm spry as a cricket this winter, though I've had some realgy (her word for rheumatism) sometimes. You know, I have had many a good bite of food in your own ma's kitchen. I owe you all a good meal."

We didn't protest anymore. We sat in awed silence, gazing with curiosity about the room. The walls were nearly covered with a motley assortment of pictures and advertisements.

We had heard a lot about Peg's pets, and now we saw them. There were six cats in the room. Four of the cats had claimed a cozy corner for their own. Another one of them, looking like a black goblin, blinked from the center of Peg's bed. Another striped beastie had both ears and one eye gone. He glared at us from the sofa in the corner. The dog, with only three legs, lay behind the stove. A crow sat on a roost above our heads in company with an old hen.

Soon tea was ready. It was not a pleasant meal in more ways than one. Things were none too clean, but we ate them. Peg was not careful of anyone's feelings.

Peg looked at Felicity with a piercing glance. "You're good-looking—but you're proud. Your complexion won't stay the same as it is now. It'll be like your ma's yet. You got too much red in your face."

Then she looked at Cecily. "You look delicate. I dare say you'll never live to grow up."

Cecily's lips trembled and Dan's face turned crimson. "Hush," he said to Peg. "You've no business to say such things to people."

I think my jaw dropped. I know Peter's and Felix's did. Felicity broke in wildly.

"Oh, don't mind him, Miss Bowen. He's got *such* a temper. That's just the way he talks to all of us at home. Please excuse him."

"Bless you, I don't mind him," said Peg. "I like a lad with lots of spirit. And so your father run away, did he, Peter," she said as she passed him some tea. "He was older than me and took me home from singing school three times when we were young. Do you know where he is now?"

"No," said Peter.

"Well, he's coming home before long," said Peg mysteriously.

"Who told you that?" cried Peter in amazement.

"I just know things," responded Peg.

If she meant to make the flesh creep on our bones, she succeeded. But now, much to our relief, the meal was over. Peg invited us to draw our chairs around the stove again.

"Make yourselves at home," she said, producing her pipe from her pocket. "I ain't one of the kind that thinks their house is too good to live in. Guess I won't bother washing the dishes. They'll do you for breakfast—if you don't forget your places."

An uncomfortable silence followed until it was broken by Peg. She introduced us to her pets and told us how she had come by them. The black cat was her favorite.

"That cat knows more than I do, if you'll believe it," she said proudly. "I got a rat too, but he's a bit shy when strangers is around. Your cat got all right again that time he was sick, didn't he?"

"Yes," said the Story Girl, remembering the day we had come to see Peg Bowen when our Paddy cat was sick.

"Thought he would," said Peg. "I seen to that. Now don't you all be staring at that hole in my dress."

"We weren't," we protested.

"Looked like you were. I tore that yesterday, but I didn't mend it yet. I was brought up to believe that a hole was an accident but a patch was a disgrace. And so your Aunt Olivia is going to be married after all."

Her words hit us like a bomb. This was news to us. We felt and looked dazed.

"I never heard anything of it," said the Story Girl. "And I live with her."

"Oh, it's true enough. She's a great fool. I've no faith in husbands. How's your missionary quilt comin' along, Cecily?"

We couldn't believe it. Was there anything Peg didn't know about us?

"Very well," said Cecily.

"You can put my name on it if you want to," said Peg.

"Oh, thank you. Which section—the five-cent one or the ten-cent one?" asked Cecily timidly.

"Well, the ten-cent one, of course. The best is none too good for me. I'll give you the ten cents another time. I'm short of change right now—not being as rich as old Queen Victoria."

Suddenly, she jumped up and said, "Well, I guess you're all sleepy and ready for bed. The girls can sleep in my bed over there, and I'll take the sofie. Yes, you can put that cat off if you like, though he won't hurt you. You boys can go downstairs. There's a big pile of straw there that will do you for a bed if you put your coats on. I'll light you down, but I ain't gonna leave a candle down there for fear you'd set fire to the place."

Saying good night to the girls, who looked like their last hour had come, we went to our room. It was quite empty save for a pile of firewood and another of clean straw. We four boys snuggled down in the straw. We didn't expect to sleep, but we were so tired that before we knew it, our eyes were shut.

The poor girls were not so fortunate. They all said that they never closed an eye. Three things kept them from sleeping—Peg snored loudly, and her pillows and bed clothes smelled of tobacco smoke. They were worried that Peg's rat might come out to make their friendship. They were sure they had heard him rooting around several times.

The next morning when we woke up, the storm was over. A young morning was looking through rosy eyelids across a white world. The little clearing around Peg's cabin was heaped with drifts, and we boys went outside and shoveled her a path out to the road. She gave us breakfast—stiff oatmeal porridge, hot milk, and a boiled egg apiece. Cecily could not eat her porridge. She declared that she had such a bad cold that she had no appetite. The rest of us choked our messes down. After we had done so, Peg asked if we had noticed a soapy taste.

"The soap fell in the porridge while I was makin' it," she said. "But," smacking her lips, "I'm gonna make you an Irish stew for dinner. It's gonna be fine."

An Irish stew concocted by Peg?

No wonder Dan said, "You're kind, but we must go right home."

"You can't walk," said Peg.

"Oh, yes we can! The drifts are so hard that they will carry us, and the snow will be pretty well blown off in the middle of the fields. It's only three-quarters of a mile."

"Seems to me you weren't in such a hurry to leave last night," said Peg sarcastically.

"Oh, it's only because they'll be so anxious about us at home, and it's Sunday. We don't want to miss Sunday school," exclaimed Felicity.

"Well, I hope your Sunday school will do you good," said Peg rather grumpily.

"We are really thankful for all your trouble," said the Story Girl politely.

"Never mind the trouble. The expense is the thing," retorted Peg grimly.

"Oh," Felicity hesitated, "if you would let us pay you, give you something? We'd be glad to."

"No, thank you," responded Peg. "There's people who take money for their hospitality, but I'm thankful to say that I don't associate with that class. You're welcome to all that you've had here, even if you are in a big hurry to get away."

Then, with no further ado, we quickly gathered our things, bundled up, and said our good-byes.

Peg shut the door behind us with something of a slam, and her black cat followed us so far that we were frightened of it. Eventually it turned back. Not until then did we feel free to discuss our adventure.

"Well, I'm glad we're out of that! Hasn't it been an awful experience?" said Felicity.

"We might have all been frozen stark and stiff this morning," remarked the Story Girl. "I tell you, it was a lucky thing we got to Peg Bowen's."

"Miss Marwood says there's no such thing as luck. We ought to say it was Providence or the Lord helped us instead," said Cecily.

"Well Peg and the Lord don't seem to go together very well somehow," said Dan.

"Do you suppose your father is really coming home like she said?" asked Felicity.

"I hope not," said Peter.

"You ought to be ashamed of yourself," said Felicity severely.

"No, I shouldn't. Father got drunk all the time he was home and wouldn't work. He was mean to mother," said Peter defiantly. "She had to support him as well as herself and me. I don't want to see my father come home, and you'd better believe it. Of course, if he were the right sort of a father, it would be different."

"What I would like to know is if Aunt Olivia is going to be married," said the Story Girl. "I can hardly believe it. But now that I think of it, Uncle Roger has been teasing her ever since she was in Halifax last summer."

"If she does get married, you'll have to come and live with us," said Cecily delightedly to the Story Girl.

Felicity didn't seem to be as happy about that, and the Story Girl remarked with a weary little sigh that she hoped Aunt Olivia wouldn't. We were all weary. Peg's predictions had been unsettling, and our nerves had been greatly strained during our time there. We were glad when we finally arrived at home.

The folks had not been at all troubled about us. They were sure that we had stayed at Cousin Mattie's. Aunt Janet raised her eyebrows when she learned where we had spent the night, but Uncle Roger said that we looked none the worse for wear.

Aunt Janet's cooking had never tasted so good as it did that night, and the woodstove had never seemed to put out as much warmth. We were quiet that night, thankful to be safe from the storm, and thankful especially to be together.

**Lucy Maud Montgomery**

1908

# Lucy Maud Montgomery
### 1874-1942

*Anne of Green Gables* was the very first book that Lucy Maud Montgomery published. In all, she wrote twenty-five books.

Lucy Maud Montgomery was born on Prince Edward Island. Her family called her Maud. Before she was two years old, her mother died and she was sent to live with her mother's parents on their farm on the Island. Her grandparents were elderly and very strict. Maud lived with them for a long time.

When she was seven, her father remarried. He moved far out west to Saskatchewan, Canada, with his new wife. At age seventeen, she went to live with them, but she did not get along with her stepmother. So she returned to her grandparents.

She attended college and studied to become a teacher—just like Anne in the Avonlea series. When her grandfather died, Maud went home to be with her grandmother. Living there in the quiet of Prince Edward Island, she had plenty of time to write. It was during this time that she wrote her first book, *Anne of Green Gables*. When the book was finally accepted, it was published soon after. It was an immediate hit, and Maud began to get thousands of letters asking for more stories about Anne. She wrote *Anne of Avonlea, Chronicles of Avonlea, Anne of the Island, Anne of Windy Poplars, Anne's House of Dreams, Rainbow Valley, Anne of Ingleside,* and *Rilla of Ingleside*. She also wrote *The Story Girl* and *The Golden Road*.

When Maud was thirty-seven years old, Ewan Macdonald, the minister of the local Presbyterian Church in Canvendish, proposed marriage to her. Maud accepted and they were married. Later on they moved to Ontario where two sons, Chester and Stewart, were born to the couple.

Maud never went back to Prince Edward Island to live again. But when she died in 1942, she was buried on the Island, near the house known as Green Gables.

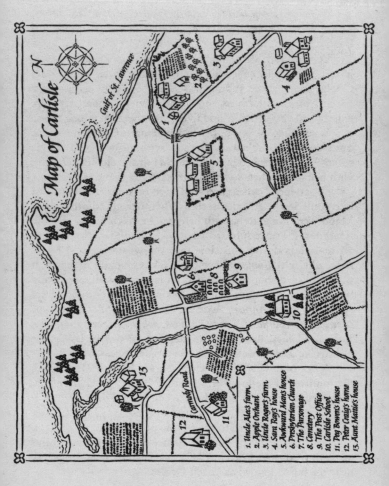

Map of Carlisle

N

Gulf of St. Lawrence

Carmody Road

1. Uncle Alec's farm
2. Apple Orchard
3. Uncle Roger's farm
4. Sam Ray's house
5. Awkward Man's house
6. Presbyterian Church
7. The Parsonage
8. Cemetery
9. The Post Office
10. Carlisle School
11. Peg Bowen's house
12. Peter Craig's home
13. Aunt Mattie's house

### The King Cousins

(Book 1)
By L.M. Montgomery
Adapted by Barbara Davoll

### Measles, Mischief, and Mishaps

(Book 2)
By L.M. Montgomery
Adapted by Barbara Davoll

Sara Stanley, the Story Girl, can captivate anyone who will listen to her tales. In this first book of the series, brothers Beverley and Felix arrive on Prince Edward Island to spend the summer with their cousins on the King Homestead. These curious and imaginative children set out to find out about the existence of God. What follows are childhood antics, tall-tales, and legends from a time long past.

SOFTCOVER 0-310-70598-3

As Sara Stanley continues to spin her wonderful stories, the King Cousins get into a load of trouble. First, they convince their neighbor, Sara Ray, to disobey her mother and go to a magic lantern show with them. Then Sara Ray gets very sick with measles and the Story Girl thinks it is all her fault. Then Dan loses a baby he is watching. And if that's not enough, he defiantly eats poisonous berries and becomes very ill. Here are more childhood antics, tall-tales, and legends from a time long past.

SOFTCOVER 0-310-70599-1

*Available now at your local bookstore!*

## zonder**kidz**

# *Summer Shenanigans* (Book 3)
## By L.M. Montgomery
## Adapted by Barbara Davoll

The King cousins read a dreaded prophecy about judgment day. When they hear a mysterious, ghostly ringing bell, they are frightened nearly out of their wits, thinking it has something to do with the end of the world. They become so frightened that the Story Girl refuses to tell any more stories. This book is filled with shenanigans and rollicking summer days as the King cousins try to make the most ot their time together on Prince Edward Island.

SOFTCOVER 0-310-70600-9

*Available now at your local bookstore!*

zonder**kidz**

# *Dreams, Schemes, and Mysteries*
## (Book 4)
### By L.M. Montgomery
### Adapted by Barbara Davoll

Toward the end of the cousins' summer together on Prince Edward Island, the Story Girl has an idea for them all to do together—a preaching contest followed by a bitter-apple-eating contest. Both contests end in near disaster as Peter, a neighbor boy, falls deathly ill. The kids decide that lots of prayer and good behavior will make him well. And it works. Things quiet down until a letter arrives saying that at long last the mysterious blue chest stored at the King Homestead can be opened and its secret revealed.

SOFTCOVER 0-310-70601-7

*Available now at your local bookstore!*

## zonder**kidz**

# *Wedding Wishes and Woes*
## (Book 6)
## By L.M. Montgomery
## Adapted by Barbara Davoll

As spring roars in like a lion, the King cousins experience a whirl of adventures—not all of them fun: Dan is knocked unconscious, a boy annoys Cecily, and Sara's cat disappears. But things take a turn for the better when Aunt Olivia announces she's getting married, and Peter's once-alcoholic father proclaims he's become a Christian. Is life always this full of changes?

SOFTCOVER 0-310-70860-5

### Midnight Madness and Mayhem
(Book 7)
By L.M. Montgomery
Adapted by Barbara Davoll

### Winds of Change
(Book 8)
By L.M. Montgomery
Adapted by Barbara Davoll

The Story Girl has moved in with the King cousins now that Aunt Olivia has married and moved to Nova Scotia. But just when it seems as if things are getting back to normal, a series of adverse events have the children wondering how to get along with their neighbors, while a pair of old romantic mysteries might—or might not—be resolved. Sara knows the secret —but will she tell?

SOFTCOVER 0-310-70861-3

When a letter arrives from South America, Bev and Felix learn their father is coming for them—and he is bringing his new wife-to-be! To add to the excitement, Sara is surprised when her father returns from Paris. Soon this large family will be scattered, so the cousins try to make the most of their remaining time together. What will life on the Island be like without the Story Girl?

SOFTCOVER 0-310-70862-1

*Available now at your local bookstore!*

**zonderkidz**

# zonder**kidz**.

We want to hear from you. Please send your comments
about this book to us in care of zreview@zondervan.com. Thank you.

Grand Rapids, MI 49530
www.zonderkidz.com